# Kids ask WHO?



**WHO** is the tallest animal on earth?

**WHO** flew the first airplane?

**WHO** was the first person to walk on the moon?

sequoia™
children's publishing

Illustrated by Marilee Harrald-Pilz

Photography © Shutterstock 2021 Vadim Sadovski; Aphelleon; jennyt; lunamarina; Eric Isselee; jaroslava V; Willyam Bradberry; Cherdchai charasri; Hung Chung Chih; Fer Gregory; CGi Heart
Photography by Brian Warling Photography and Siede Preis Photography

Published by Sequoia Children's Publishing,
a division of Phoenix International Publications, Inc.

8501 West Higgins Road
Chicago, Illinois 60631

59 Gloucester Place
London W1U 8JJ

Heimhuder Straße 81
20148 Hamburg



Customer Service: cs@sequoiakidsbooks.com



www.sequoiakidsbooks.com

ISBN 978-1-64269-353-9

Kids ask

# WHO?

## Table of Contents

# WHO was the first person to walk on the moon?

Three astronauts went to the moon in 1969. **Neil Armstrong** walked on the moon first. **Buzz Aldrin** came next. **Michael Collins** stayed in the ship to help Neil and Buzz.

## Did you know?

Thousands of people worked together on Earth to help the astronauts get to the moon. Three of those people are **Mary Jackson**, **Katherine Johnson**, and **Dorothy Vaughan**. They won awards for their work. A movie was made about them.

# **WHO** flew the first airplane?

**Wilbur and Orville Wright** were brothers. They invented the airplane. Their first flight was on December 17, 1903. They kept working to make planes better and better.

## Did you know?

**Amelia Earhart** was famous for flying planes in the 1930s. She loved taking long, exciting flights. She wrote books and helped other women who wanted to fly planes.

# WHO invented Halloween?

In ancient times, people in Europe had their New Year on October 31. They dressed up as animals. Treats were left out for ghosts.

# WHO invented gum?

People have chewed gum for thousands of years. Gum was made from sticky tree sap or tree resin. Today, gum is made by people, not trees.

## Did you know?

People in Mexico and Central America invented chocolate. In ancient times, they mixed water, spices, and roasted cacao beans. They had chocolate as a drink.

# WHO is the "King of the Beasts"?

Some people call the lion the "King of the Beasts." Lions are big, strong, and beautiful. They look majestic. Male lions have hair around their head called a mane. Their mane looks like a crown.

## Did you know?

Some lions weigh as much as nine first-graders!

## WHO is the tallest animal on Earth?

The giraffe is the tallest animal on Earth. It is as tall as a two-story house! It has very long legs and a very long neck. Giraffes can eat leaves high up in trees. They can see things from far away.

# **WHO** was one of the best teachers ever?

There have been a lot of amazing teachers! One was **Anne Sullivan**. Anne taught a little girl named **Helen Keller**. Helen could not hear or see. Anne taught Helen to understand things with her hands. She taught Helen to use her hands to speak. Helen became a famous writer and speaker.

## Did you know?

Braille is a kind of writing that uses raised dots. People who cannot see can feel the dots. They can read with their fingers!

# WHO created basketball?

In 1891, a teacher named **Dr. James Naismith** needed a game his students could play in wintertime. The game had to be safe to play inside. It had to tire people out. James came up with basketball!

## Did you know?

James taught at a school for young men. A year after James invented basketball, a teacher named **Senda Berenson** read about the new game. She taught her students the game. They were all young women.

# WHO built the longest wall in the world?

The Great Wall of China is the longest wall in the world. It was built by many, many people. It was built over two thousand years. It could stretch from Chicago to Paris!

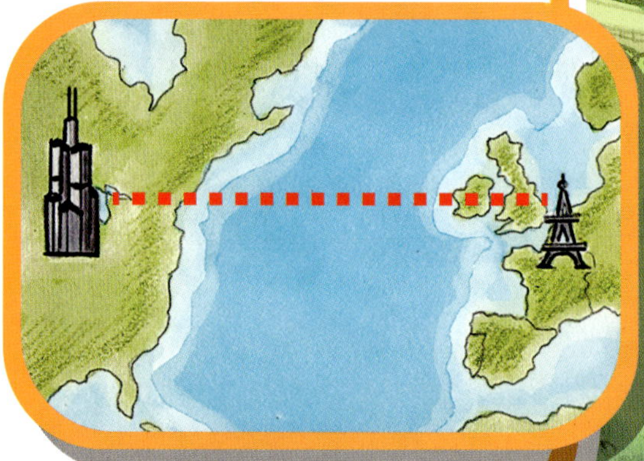

## Did you know?

The Great Wall started out as many smaller walls. The oldest parts are almost 2,500 years old.

## WHO first used x-ray machines?

Doctors started using x-rays to help people in 1895. But **Marie Curie** might have helped the most people. She was a scientist. During World War I, she put x-ray machines in cars. She trained 150 women to use them. The women drove to battlefields. They helped over a million soldiers.

## WHO invented the cast?

About 1,000 years ago, a doctor named **Al-Zahrawi** wrote about making a cast out of flour and egg white. The mixture makes a hard cover when it dries.

## Did you know?

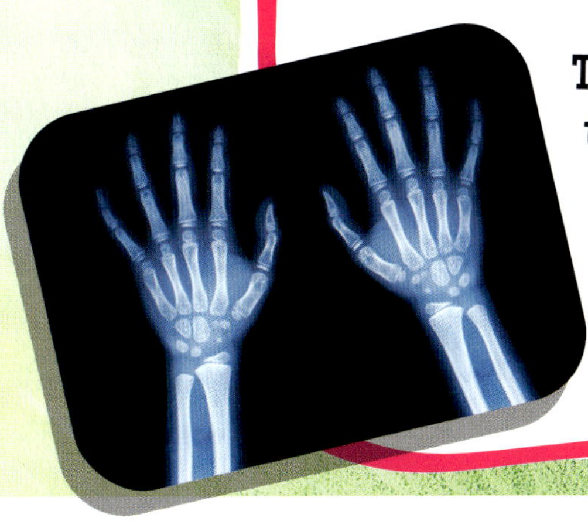

Think about how light goes through a window. That is sort of how x-rays go through our bodies. When we get an x-ray, doctors can see in our bodies to help us.

# WHO takes my bag when I fly on an airplane?

When you give a worker at the airport your bag, they put a tag on it. The tag says where you are going. Another worker looks at the tag and takes the bag out to your plane. Your bag is on your plane with you! You just can't see it.